The Butterfly Man & Other Stories

The Butterfly Man & Other Stories
Mehis Heinsaar
Translated from the Estonian
by Adam Cullen and Tiina Randviir

The Butterfly Man & Other Stories by Mehis Heinsaar
This edition has been published in 2018 in the United Kingdom by Paper + Ink

PAPER

+ INK

www.paperand.ink
Twitter: @paper_andink
Instagram: paper_and.ink

The stories featured in this edition were first published in Estonian as
"Liblikmees" ("The Butterfly Man") by Tuum in 2001; *"Kaunitar, kes oli
kõike juba näinud Ühe elukunstniku jutustus"* ("The Beauty Who Had
Seen It All") by Menu Kirjastus in 2010; and *"Suur Hooaeg"*
("The High Season") by Verb in 2007.

English translation of *"Liblikmees"* © Tiina Randviir, 2017
English translation of *"Kaunitar, kes oli kõike juba näinud
Ühe elukunstniku jutustus"* and *"Suur Hooaeg"* © Adam Cullen, 2018

1 2 3 4 5 6 7 8 9 10

ISBN 9781911475354

This book has been translated and published with support from the
Estonian Cultural Endowment's Traducta translation programme
and its "English Wallet" financing programme.

EESTI KULTUURKAPITAL

A CIP catalogue record for this book is available from the British Library.
Jacket design by James Nunn: www.jamesnunn.co.uk | @Gnunkse
Printed and bound in Poland by Opolgraf: www.opolgraf.com

CONTENTS

THE
BUTTERFLY
MAN

When Ansel entered the circus director's office, his jaw dropped in amazement: it seemed to him that the man sitting at the desk, there in front of him, had the head of a fish! But it must only have been a trick of the eye, because in the next second, a perfectly normal man, small, fat and bald, began yelling at him:

"How dare you come into my office without knocking? What cheek! It says on the door that I'm having lunch, doesn't it?

Who do you think you are, and what do you want, may I ask? Or better not – just get the hell out of here!"

Anselm was not going to give in so easily; he was determined to get a job at the Boruslawski Magic Circus.

"I'm really awfully sorry, sir," he said. "You are the director, I presume?" But upon seeing the man's face cloud over, he knew it was indeed Boruslawski himself. "Erm, well, Mr Boruslawski, I'll be quite frank with you: I'd like to get the conjurer's job in your circus."

On hearing this, the little man suddenly grew attentive. He quickly slipped off his chair and scurried over to Anselm, panting and staring up into his face, goggle-eyed. "Ah, so that's what you're after. Did you read the advertisement carefully?"

"I did," said Anselm, somewhat surprised by the man's suspicious gaze.

"In that case, you must have noticed that only a really skilled master stands a chance here." Suddenly the corners of the man's mouth turned up into a smile. "Perhaps you've got some document to prove your skill, or a list of tricks that you can perform?"

Anselm's voice took on a slightly less confident tone: "I don't think I have any papers," he mumbled, staring at the ground, "but I can build a house of cards in an instant, and pull pairs of rabbits out of a hat, and –"

He halted as Boruslawski's grin turned into a sneer. "Just as I thought," the circus director said. "My dear man, that's all old hat! It doesn't matter how good you are at it; rabbits, cards, all that stuff, none of it grabs audiences today. Let me tell you about our last conjurer, Ernesto. He was quite on the ball. His forte was transforming small objects – and he was a true master. For example, he could gaze at a spectator's watch until it turned into a real wagtail, or stare someone's jacket button into a copper coin – easy as pie for him! Once he even turned a lady's shoelace into a blindworm. Admittedly, the lady had a heart attack, but what a trick, eh? Ernesto's performances often dragged on until midnight, but audiences were prepared to stick it out happily, because it was real *art*. Do you understand?"

Anselm nodded in deference. "But what happened to him?"

"What happened, what happened – what usually happens in these cases! The more talent, the less brains. One evening he tried to stare a ping-pong ball into a golden globe, and suffered a stroke. Overestimated his own powers ... And now, I'm afraid, you'll have to excuse me. I'm in a bit of a hurry. There's no way I can offer you a job here; our audiences are well-educated, they'll boo you off. So, good day to you."

Nobody in this world needs me anymore, thought Anselm in despair. *To tell the truth, Boruslawski is quite right to throw me out.*

Downcast, he turned to go. As he touched the door handle, something in Anselm snapped and separated from him in the form of a swarm of butterflies, scattering in all directions around the director's office. Anselm turned deathly pale and began to flap his arms about, trying to catch the fluttering creatures. In the process, he smashed a few vases and an aquarium with some goldfish in it. He stuffed the butterflies he did catch into his mouth, casting wild glances toward the circus director, who stood, petrified, watching the conjurer's every move.

"I usually have lunch at this time," was Anselm's stupid explanation. "And I want to keep to my mealtimes."

Realising how feeble this sounded, the conjurer fled the room. As he ran downstairs, he heard someone hyperventilating behind him, and ran faster. At the front door, however, Boruslawski caught up with the fugitive. "Hey, what's the big hurry? What you just showed me, all those butterflies – that was brilliant!"

"... Oh, please ... don't mock my disability," replied Anselm. "I've suffered enough already. It's always the same; every time I experience a strong emotion, these creatures start flying off my body. I was bullied at school for it, and my relatives, even my parents, saw me as some kind of freak, although I've always been of perfectly sound mind.

"The only one who ever took an interest in my phenomenon was a maniac biologist – a perverse interest. Actually, she became my lover in order to examine me more thoroughly. Among my body butterflies she found marsh carpets and bagworm moths, but she took a particular fancy to the purple emperors that emerged when I experienced physical ecstasy. She counted over five hundred species, each supposedly indicating a particular mood of mine. I finally got fed up with her nonsense, and sent her packing. So now you know."

"But it's simply fantastic!" Boruslawski exclaimed, overjoyed. "Your biologist was a gem, and you, my dear young friend, are a great magician. Tomorrow you shall be our star attraction – if you're happy with that, of course – and your salary will be triple what we're offering! Come and meet your wonderful colleagues, who will show you your quarters."

The flushed director dragged Anselm to

the back rooms and pressed an unexpectedly large sum of money into his hand. "This is an advance. Irmgiird!" he shouted. "Come show our young magician his new home!" Borulawski made a slight bow, and left.

Irmgiird turned out to be a huge woman, possibly more than three metres tall. Her thick, red hair was tied back in a ponytail, and her smile revealed a row of sharp, white teeth. "Irmgiird, lion tamer," she introduced herself in a low, purring voice, and held out a scratched hand.

"Glad to meet you. I'm Anselm, mediocre conjurer, and I suppose you can now call me 'The Butterfly Man' too," muttered Anselm, staring foolishly at his feet. Smiling, Irmgiird took him by the arm, and the odd couple went to explore the backstage area.

Anselm saw a weird selection of people there: it was rather like wandering into a dream world. He saw a man with a transparent body surrounded by gorgeous women with non-transparent bodies, who seemed to form his harem; he saw an old, wrinkled woman with a long, white horn growing out of her forehead, whose sweet breath reminded Anselm of a long-forgotten world. Two children with wings for arms floated near the ceiling; their flight resembled that of bats. There was also a troupe of acrobats practising various routines, who were distinctive in that their skin was covered with fish scales. Countless attendants bustled around everywhere, ready to satisfy the *artistes'* every whim.

Anselm felt acutely uneasy as he moved through this company, and it grew more difficult for him to work out whether this was just a collection of freaks from different parts of the world, or rare and wonderful creatures whose ranks he now had the honour of joining. When Irmgiird asked him what he thought of his new colleagues, he shrugged shyly and replied: "Maybe I would be better off as a mediocre conjurer somewhere else – it's rather intimidating here."

This comment really made Irmgiird fly off the handle. She grabbed Anselm by the collar and clasped him between her magnificent breasts. "You're just a stupid little shithead to talk like that," she rasped viciously. "Do you think I'm some kind of monster, too? Maybe I should be ashamed of my might and beauty, is that it?"

For the duration of this tirade, Anselm was forced to look into her dark green eyes and breathe in the heady smell of musk emanating from between her breasts. Suddenly, a huge cloud of emperor butterflies burst forth from him, the telltale sign of supreme ecstasy.

Seeing this, Irmgiird immediately relented, squatted down in front of Anselm and spoke in a much softer tone: "Tell me, Butterfly Man, why are you ashamed of your peculiarity? Why pretend to be a dumb charlatan when, clearly, you are not? Your place is here with us. Out there, we are all regarded as freaks and cripples – but here, we are admired as demigods. Come, I'll show you your rooms."

Irmgiird took hold of Anselm's hand as if he were a little child, and led him to his new home. It seemed rather luxurious; he was even assigned two bald attendants. (One immediately started polishing his shoes, and the other brushed his jacket.) Before leaving, the huge woman bent down and whispered into Anselm's ear that she would wait for him in her room after the following day's performance. At once, four or five Dewick's plusias (*Macdunnoughia confusa*) detached themselves from Anselm – indicating the utter confusion in the Butterfly Man's soul.

It was only after midnight that the former conjurer fell into a nightmarish and delirious sleep. His life, after all, had taken such an unexpected turn. At some point he saw himself staggering into the arena in the form of a huge beetle while the audience, consisting of man-sized bugs and centipedes, waited impatiently for his performance. Anselm started to peel off his disgusting black shell until he was standing in the middle of the arena, a shivering, naked young man. Suddenly the audience rose up, stormed the arena and began to devour him greedily. Fortunately, he had forgotten the bad dream by the time he woke in the morning – but a childish fear stayed with him, a premonition that all would not be quite as simple as expected at the evening performance.

To calm his nerves, Anselm went for a stroll around town; but on every street corner, wherever he went, he saw huge posters announcing the circus:

WELCOME TO THE MAGIC CIRCUS!
EVERY ACT IS A WONDER OF THE WORLD!
STAR ATTRACTION:
THE BUTTERFLY MAN!
WORLD-FAMOUS ENTOMOLOGIST
PROFESSOR AMIRGALDI
WILL BE PRESENT TO IDENTIFY
PREVIOUSLY UNSEEN SPECIES!
COME! YOU WON'T REGRET IT!

At every poster, two or three Baltic graylings (*Oeneis jutta*) detached themselves from Anselm, denoting ordinary fright, and soon he was forced to return to the circus so as not to attract too much attention to himself.

As the evening progressed, Anselm's fear turned into an overwhelming apathy toward everything around him. Before the performance, he chose an unremarkable tailcoat at least three sizes too big, and a totally ill-suited, silly cap with a long peak. The attendants watched him anxiously, but did not dare interfere. Anselm then took up his position behind the curtain and waited his turn, sinking slowly into a deepening torpor.

Suddenly, as if from nowhere, the circus director himself appeared, all flushed and breathing hard, accompanied by a spindly man wearing a pince-nez who immediately started examining Anselm with the utmost care. Boruslawski said: "May I introduce Professor Amirgaldi – hang on, what on Earth are you wearing? You don't look anything like a magician! But I suppose you know what you're doing. You're on in seven minutes." Then he was gone, leaving the sharp-eyed professor and the completely expressionless Anselm staring at each other.

In order to get out of this embarrassing situation, the Butterfly Man sauntered over to the curtain and peered out at the arena. Irmgiird, in a sparkling leotard, was just finishing her routine with the lions – she really would have made a perfect wife for Hercules. The circus was packed; the advertisements had worked. There was the applause already ... now it was Anselm's turn.

A flushed Irmgiird rushed past the Butterfly Man with two lions, and blew him a happy kiss. When Anselm, the professor and the attendants appeared in the arena, they were greeted with roaring applause. This did not shake Anselm's indifference; he sat down on a chair in the middle of the ring, crossed his legs and fixed his eyes on his right shoe.

The crowd went absolutely silent.

"Well, well," thought Anselm, smiling to himself, "today they are going to see the wittiest performance in the world – a 'miracle man' who just sits on a chair for a while with his legs crossed, then walks away." For a moment, such a spectacle even seemed rather interesting.

In the meantime, the attendants were anxiously hovering around Anselm, and Professor Amirgaldi, holding a tin megaphone at his lips, was poised to yell out the Latin names of the butterflies; but the Butterfly Man just sat on his chair, his face a blank, swinging his right leg like a wind-up doll. An hour passed. The audience was still quiet – but for how long?

Suddenly the circus director, who was sitting in the front row, stood up in agitation. Beckoning an attendant, he whispered something in his ear. The attendant rushed back to the other with a conspiratorial look on his face. This activity in the arena caught the attention of the audience, and they began fidgeting in anticipation.

Each attendant took a small object from his pocket: a quill, half an onion, a small pair of pincers. They gathered around Anselm and tried to make him laugh or cry – anything to bring him out of this defiant mood. However, they achieved nothing more than a few silly giggles.

Some of the spectators now began to think that this was, in fact, a mummified Butterfly Man whom the others were trying to revive, and they applauded enthusiastically at every sound Anselm produced. Others, however, frowned at them knowingly, indicating that they had got it all wrong.

A few more hours went by without

anything special happening. The audience, although well-trained in waiting for miracles, grew restless. Then came the first catcalls. Some people walked out with contemptuous grimaces on their faces. However, most of the audience – which was made up largely of natural scientists of varying degrees of competence – decided to stay put, just to see how it would all end. Among them were Irmgiird, who looked most unhappy, and Boruslawski, who sat slumped and desolate in his seat.

By midnight, Anselm had sunk into a deep sleep. He dreamed of himself as a small boy lying in a meadow in springtime, his hands clasped behind his head. Everything was rosy. That gossamer vision appeared so vividly to the Butterfly Man that he knew for certain – right there and then – that he had never actually existed before or after that day.

Inflamed by this idea, a swarm of yellow-line quakers erupted from Anselm's body, denoting rapture over such an unexpected *idée fixe*. The sight startled Professor Amirgaldi, who had been falling asleep himself from boredom and exhaustion. He jumped up and started yelling into his megaphone: *"Agrochola macilenta! Fantastico! Agrochola macilenta!"* People in the audience were getting to their feet, too, and deafening applause filled the house.

But that was just the beginning. The dream had made it clear to Anselm that compared to that faraway day, his entire subsequent life was nothing more than meaningless shadow theatre. He slipped into such a chaotic state of mind that he lost all control of himself. The full spectrum of his emotions burst forth in hundreds of species of *Lepidoptera*, so that in no time at all his entire body became obscured. Brush-footed butterflies mingled with bagworm moths; yellow-white butterflies fluttered around with autumn silkworm moths; swarms of false owlet moths blended into swarms of burnet moths – and all these thousands of tiny, gliding creatures expressed the joys, sorrows and thoughts of Anselm's past and future days.

At the sight of such a fierce outbreak of colour, the mood of the audience became increasingly euphoric. Spectators tearfully hugged those standing next to them, or produced bottles of wine from their coat pockets and downed the contents in one go. Everybody tried to respond to Anselm's miracle in his or her own way. The circus director was overjoyed; he leaped from his seat and did a somersault, which was most unexpected, given his bulky frame.

This dramatic outburst of joy immediately earned him a separate round of applause. Only Irmgiird stood, strangely sombre and quiet, in the midst of the jubilant crowd and watched Anselm's transformation with an anxious expression.

Professor Amirgaldi was jumping up and down around the multitude of butterflies, under which a man was presumably still sitting; he shouted new Latin insect names into his megaphone – *"Sideridis reticulata! Hadena confusa! Amphipoea!"* – until his voice grew hoarse and finally broke off altogether. Several knowledgeable people immediately emerged from the crowd, rushed into the arena and milled around in a highly agitated manner, shouting riotously. (They were far less proficient than Professor Amirgaldi, of course.) The world-famous expert did not like this at all. Brandishing the megaphone, he attempted to herd the amateur busybodies out of the arena and back to their seats. His efforts generated even greater confusion, so that it all came to resemble a fairground free-for-all.

At a certain point, though, all the noise and excitement subsided as people began to notice that there was now a disturbingly high number of butterflies in the building – and still more and more were emerging from Anselm's body. The entire arena was already quite full of the colourful, floating creatures. There was hardly any more breathing space. Desperately seeking a way out, the butterflies squeezed into people's mouths and eyes, and cries of admiration now turned into sneezes and shrieks. This particular miracle seemed somewhat too overwhelming and frightening for most.

Irmgiird, now more worried than ever,

tapped her large finger on the still-exultant circus director's bald skull and whispered into his ear that she thought all was not well with Anselm. Boruslawski duly looked around at the raging chaos with a more sober eye, and his pale pink pate slowly turned bright red.

"Anselm! Stop it immediately, do you hear? Or I'll sack you!"

This, in fact, is only what Boruslawski had intended to yell; but the instant he opened his mouth, a dozen or so scorched-wing butterflies (denoting passionate abandon on Anselm's scale of emotions) rushed into his windpipe. Irmgiird had to give him quite a few slaps on the back to prevent the distinguished man from asphyxiating. Pulling himself together, Boruslawski forced his way into the arena through the dense swarms of butterflies, and stretched out his hands to where the conjurer's body should have been; but the only thing he managed to get hold of was a throbbing human heart – and even that gradually turned into wildly fluttering butterflies in his hands. Precisely at that moment, Boruslawski – let it be noted here that he had once been one of the most famous and sought-after conjurers in the world, whose main trick was turning himself into the primeval coelacanth fish, but he later lost faith in himself and set up the present, unique circus as a consolation – was seized with genuine bewilderment and, at the same time, seething envy, for here was a man who had exceeded his wildest fantasies in the field of metamorphosis.

In the meantime, the circus attendants had had the presence of mind to open all the doors and windows, so most of the butterflies and people had already poured out of the suffocating building and into the waking city.

Swarms of butterflies soon covered the entire sky above the city. The people coming from the circus filled the streets, causing much excitement among sleepy citizens on their way to work.

Only a few especially enthusiastic ento-mologists remained in the building – among them Professor Amirgaldi, who was now running around between rows of seats trying to catch the rarer species of butterfly, or those that had not actually even been discovered yet.

On the chair where Anselm had been sitting just an hour earlier, there now lay a crumpled tailcoat and a peaked hat. Boruslawski was still standing behind the chair, his sad coelacanth eyes following the flight of the last butterfly. It was an Amanda's blue that circled around the arena a few times and then landed on Irmgiird's shoulder as she stood by a window. The giant woman eyed the insect's iridescent light blue wings, and reckoned that perhaps this was Anselm's true self, a millionth part of the conjurer, finally free of the entire disconcerting web of emotions housed by the human body; maybe now he wanted to tell her something momentous, something that he could not or did not know how to say before ...

But then the morning breeze snatched the butterfly away, and Irmgiird soon lost sight of it.

THE BEAUTY
WHO HAD
SEEN IT ALL

This story took place in the town of Pärnu, during the last days of my youth. I'd found work as a night watchman at the old river harbour that summer, and given that my days were free, I spent them strolling along the beach promenade or down the boulevards. On the rare occasion I was feeling a bit cocky, I would try hitting on girls in restaurants – but these pursuits were always unsuccessful. The freshness I'd once had had worn from my face, and the signs of a life lived hard and fast stood out too starkly for any of the targets to take me seriously. Even so, I didn't complain. My life had reached the point of chilly midday, at which earlier backfires of all kinds have already tempered you, and you're able to gaze upon your failings with philosophical tranquillity. I'd begun to realise that the greatest art in life is to learn how to be a simple or perhaps even a pointless man, capable of taking pleasure in frivolous escapades and feeling chipper about it all the same.

Testament to my progress in this difficult art might, for instance, be the fact that earlier in the evening I shall relate here, I had closed my eyes in bliss as I listened to the blackbirds sing along the boulevard that leads down to the beach, cradling in my heart a delicate joy that sprang from the state of being alive, from breathing and existing in the first place. I felt morning clouds drifting by under my eyelids.

Rousing myself from this euphoric languor and strolling leisurely onward, I happened to pass a second-hand store on the ground floor of a wooden house; as the nights were already becoming chilly, I reckoned I would buy myself an inexpensive hat.

I entered the shop, and the seller kindly directed me to a crate in the corner that was heaped high with scarves, gloves and hats. One after another, I tried on all sorts of baseball caps, brimmed hats and berets – but none seemed to suit me, for some reason. Maybe it was that my head was too big; maybe it was pickiness. In any case, standing in front of the mirror, I cocked them this way and that on my head, until all of a sudden ...

I was gone. Whether or not you looked in the mirror, I was simply gone!

What the hell! I thought in astonishment,

and was about to start yelling for help when, in a flash, my reflection reappeared in the mirror. I was holding a midnight-blue beret. I stared at my reflection, and then at the hat clenched in my hand. I placed the beret back on my head. And ... I disappeared again!

I removed the beret, and I was back in the mirror once more. Only then did I realise it was a bona fide magic hat. Naturally, I felt my lungs inflate with joy, ready to cry out and cheer at the thought, because miracles aren't at all common in our day and age! I walked over to the cashier, paid the two euros for the hat and left, humming softly.

My heart bursting with nervous and joyful disquiet, I realised that something like finding a magic hat rewinds a person's makeup to at least ten years younger – thus I no longer had any use for philosophical peace of mind. I stuck my fingers down my throat, retched that peace of mind out into my hand, and flung it over a fence.

"Now, I've got whole days full of things to do!" I rejoiced inwardly.

Having impatiently endured my overnight hours in the watchman's booth at the old river harbour, I bolted straight into town the next morning, donned my invisibility beret and began passing the time as amusingly as my mediocre abilities could possibly allow.

I pinched the butts of a few pretty salesgirls, causing them to squeal at the top of their lungs; at a local café, I gorged on sweet rum balls to the bursting point; I nabbed a wiener from a drunk Finnish tourist's plate and swallowed it right in front of him as he roared in terror. I helped myself to grilled chicken, art books and expensive herbal liqueurs from various stores; I walked around the women's-only nude beach area, inspecting their bare chests with interest; I got away with a lot of other tomfoolery. When night finally fell and I was still pretty amped up from all my mischief, I decided to treat myself to some drinks at the beach restaurant before heading to my overnight shift. And this is where the story truly begins.

It was looking like that – hands on my hips, wearing a midnight-blue magic beret on my head and brimming with youthful vigour – that I entered the second-floor beach bar on that fateful night to check out the scene.

Soft music was playing; couples pressed against one another glided across the dance floor; and the southern red sunset glittering across the Bay of Pärnu spilled in through the windows. The barman, who had combed-back, gelled hair and a cloying smile, was busy serving bikinied beauties and potbellied businessmen. It was the bar of the rich and the beautiful.

Obviously, I revelled in the anticipation of treating myself to pricy liquor at the expense of a crowd as vacuous as that. Of course, I did have to be very careful that no one saw the floating bottle of whiskey or the floating glass into which I poured its contents. Luckily, everyone had their hands much too full to notice anything soaring through the air.

So, a glass of good old Johnnie Walker in hand, I finally took a seat by the windows, near an athletic-looking man and two women.

I'll note straight away that one of the women was a true beauty. Observing her furtively, a long-held conviction of mine became even more deeply entrenched: that as far as humans go, the natural masterpieces of this world are particularly and in no unclear terms women ... An elusive shade of sorrow was painted across this elfishly attractive young woman's elegant face; the melancholic tenderness of her eyelids, cheekbones and eyebrows conjured up Botticelli's *The Birth of Venus*, and her glinting eyes, which resembled azure springs, wandered somewhere far in the distance, resembling those of a woman awaiting a sailor's return. And her figure – oh, better not to mention it at all! The god who had shaped a body the likes of hers must have had an exceptional sense of form.

The aspect that caused men to fall in love with this woman in a split second lay, perhaps, in the unconcealed sexuality of her body and the simultaneous angelic vulnerability of her expression. She looked like a young Madonna, only five times more gorgeous. I simply lack the words to praise her beauty!

Nevertheless, the athletic man sitting next to that beauty appeared to be a total lost cause. He might have been strong, rich and handsome at some point, but he had since turned into a wet rag. His eyes were red and baggy from insomnia, and he was wheezing and chain-smoking. His hands trembled, and the look in his eyes was that of a dog on a chain, irrevocably infatuated with his transcendent fairy. Truly, there is no worse fate than to be hopelessly in love with a beauty who is hopelessly tired of you. For that is the very point their relationship appeared to have reached.

The beauty, taking no notice of her admirer's puppy-dog eyes, was complaining to her friend in a soft, musical voice: "Honey, if you only knew how miserable my life is. I've already seen all this world has to offer.

I've dated Scotland's most talented poet and The Netherlands' richest architect; I've been adored by the French ambassador, the singer Jaan Tätte and the theatre director Elmo Nüganen. The Lithuanian stuntman Juris Vasiliauskas performed his infamous kamikaze flight after I declined his marriage proposal ... If you only knew how burdensome it all is! I've shed tears over my own beauty and over the men who've lost their minds because of me, but as it stands, my soul is callous and my tears have run out. I've already seen it all, over my lifetime. Nothing can surprise me anymore. Oh, if only this accursed life could show me something new just one more time ..."

I choked down my emotions, so much did I want to be that man who was capable of surprising this ethereal being who sat before me with something unexpected;

but, alas, I admitted to myself that with my average looks and modest intellectual qualities, I was, more likely than not as good as invisible to her. Which, in reality, I actually was. Nevertheless, I could still take in this woman's beauty, undisturbed, sitting in her presence and listening to her lilting voice. And at first, that sufficed. When the beauty's friend finished her cigarette and started to leave, the beauty forced her puppy-dog-eyed beau to go with her.

"Darling, you know I'm bored to death with you," she said wearily. "Please go, go with her – I'm truly begging you! Maybe I'll come and meet you both later." The woebegone athlete obediently kissed her hand and departed.

Thus I was left alone with the beauty at a table drenched in evening sunlight. She gazed languidly out at the sea, alight with the glow of sunset, and I tried to do the same. But

as I was a bit tipsy, I threw caution to the wind
before long and asked the young woman:

"Would you like another Martini with a
slice of orange?"

The beauty who had already seen it all
looked back and forth, startled.

"Who's that?" she asked anxiously. "Who's
talking to me?"

"It is I, the invisible man," I replied softly
but assuredly.

At this, the beauty became even more
shocked, and even *eeped* in fright. But
when a Martini with a slice of orange did
float through the air and settle before her,
she collected her wits, took a big gulp
from the glass and peered cautiously in the
direction in which she believed I was sitting.
Tremulously, the divine young woman asked
who on Earth I was, and why I was creeping
around without any sort of an appearance.

But from the beauty's expression, I could tell that she'd garnered an interest in me – and that gave me courage.

Although I provided only vague details about myself at first, after a couple sips of whisky I managed to quickly settle into the life story I'd whipped up mere moments before. I began spinning a tale about an awful Madagascan disease that had struck me long ago: a disease that gradually – starting with my head and moving down to the soles of my feet – rendered my stunningly handsome features completely invisible. I also related the unfortunate fate that followed, forcing me to wander the world like Ahasuerus.

The beauty listened with deepening fascination, and staring into her blue eyes welling with tears, I realised that she was probably even starting to fall in love with me. With renewed gusto, I took a couple more sips of whisky and started detailing my physical appearance vividly. I sighed softly to her about how, as a child, I'd had golden locks and sea-green eyes; about how even at that early age, I sang folk songs from the Estonian islands from morning to night; about how a distinguished relative had foretold for me a future as a great poet; and so on and so forth ...

By closing time, things had progressed to the point where this divine sprite was leaning gently against my invisible body as we made our way toward the Hotel Pärnu. Oh, feeble mankind! Be joyous in your mediocrity, for you know not the hellfire that erupts in an inconsequential man when a gorgeous woman decides to fall in love with him.

When we arrived at the hotel room, the beauty who had already seen everything in life slowly undressed me and began stroking my arms, legs, and face with childlike curiosity.

You could read the innocent joy of a young girl in her expression. The woman's cheeks were flushed from the lust and yearning for what she could not see, but which she could imagine all the more graphically from what I'd described. It felt like she had begun playing with me as though with a cherished fantasy that had, at long last, become real in invisible form.

I folded my arms behind my head and allowed it all to transpire with pleasure, only forbidding her from touching my midnight-blue beret, claiming that the hat had medicinal properties that kept me from ceasing to exist entirely. Hearing this, the incredible beauty began crying out of compassion. How big and clear her tears were!

Again and again, she demanded all kinds of details about my former life and looks, and each and every time, I came up with something new: I described the colours of my skin, eyes and hair in ever more brilliant shades, and ultimately not even I could understand anymore whether, according to my new life story, I should be black, American Indian or Sámi. But the beauty who had already seen everything actually appeared to enjoy this constantly transforming appearance most of all. Her delicate fingers stroked my body, my belly and my thighs with ever-greedier fascination. Every now and then, I took a swig of whisky from the bottle to stoke my imagination, and then carried on with my descriptions, sinking deeper and deeper into my own endlessly metamorphosing appearance.

But then arrived the blessed moment: the beauty could no longer contain her lust, and asked me to undress her ... Oh, Heavenly Rollers of Dice! I shall thank you till the end of my days for those wondrous moments!

The touch of my hand unleashed a blissful and contented expression on the young woman's angelic countenance, as though she'd been touched by a god. And when she was finally lying naked next to me – golden bronzed skin, slightly parted lips, eyes gently closed in anticipation – I realised that she was giving me silent permission to do anything to her. I wondered then whether or not I, in that state, invisible and aswarm with lies, had any right to make love to her; still, looking upon her body bursting with longing and awaiting gratification, and staring at her eyes closed in bliss, I could no longer resist my blazing desire.

Even when she was relishing the pleasures of our lovemaking, the beauty insisted that I continue telling her my life story. Well, and so I did: I recounted my adventures in Jamaica and Nicaragua; I described my brush with a jaguar in the Brazilian rainforest; I spoke of my gloomy solitude in the Welsh village of Laugharne, where I wrote timeless poems in a boathouse anchored to the edge of a cliff ... I was someone completely different with every new coitus. At one point, I wove myself into her fantasies as Pushkin with his gigantic mutton chops, then made myself a beautiful beast akin to the Marquis de Sade or Yesenin, followed by a pensive American Indian or a hermetic Indian monk from somewhere on Mount Arunachala.

As a result, the ethereal beauty had five orgasms in a row in rather short intervals, and we became the wildest and happiest pair of lovers that summer!

My beloved, who had already seen everything in life, became increasingly submissive with each passing day, bringing me meals and drinks in bed. She'd have agreed to brush my teeth if I only wished it. She would gaze endlessly at my invisible face, hair and body with such tender devotion that I was almost certain our love would last like that, forever. Mutual understanding and immaculate joy flourished between us in this manner for three whole weeks.

But then, one day – just as such things always happen 'one day' – the beauty started asking whether or not there might be some kind of medicine that would make my form at least the slightest bit discernible, so that she could glimpse my face and my body, even for a mere moment. At first, I categorically ruled out the possibility. But when her pitiful moaning had lasted for days, I finally broke.

"There is!" I announced grandly one evening after we'd drunk our next bottle of champagne and had just finished trying out an extremely difficult lovemaking pose. "There is such a medicine!" So I exclaimed, and then recklessly swept the midnight-blue beret off my head.

I regretted my action bitterly a moment later, but it was too late. What followed was horrible. For the first twenty seconds or so that the beauty eyed my appearance made flesh, her eyes shone with veritable joy (I can assure you of that!), but then she seemed to realise *that* was the way I was. Just as she saw me, there. That I'd been that way before, that I was like that now, and that I'll continue being like that to the very end. Her look of desire extinguished as first proof of this realisation; then her mouth twisted into a wry smirk, and a moment later she erupted into hysterical laughter. The outburst of laughing swelled into weeping, and wild cursing as she flung things at me. She began accusing me of gross abuse, of being repugnant, of rape and God knows what all else. My attempts to calm her down only added fuel to the fire, turning her abuse into full-blown, screeching rage. I soon had no other choice but to grab my things – and my magic beret – and hightail it out of the room.

At first, I was even flooded with a certain sensation of jubilant freedom. Exhausted, I drank a beer on the beachfront promenade, watched the puffy white clouds sail by, thought back upon those happy days and let the sea breeze ruffle my hair. But that night, while thinking everything over again, sitting under the trees in the park, I realised how very deeply I loved her, all the same. And I broke down in tears.

My self-regard had shattered in a single day.

Two mornings later, I crawled back to her door like a lowly dog, but the beauty called the hotel porter and had me thrown out. After that, I tried climbing up to her room along a drainpipe, but it broke and I sprained my ankle in the fall. I attempted to get close to the young woman a few times more to win back her love, but nothing helped. I no longer interested her; quite the opposite. The beauty so much as threatened to have her athlete-admirer knock the living daylights out of me if she ever happened to see me again. In a state of absolute despair, I flung my midnight-blue beret somewhere, never to find it again.

My subsequent attempts to break into the hotel were all unsuccessful, as I wasn't permitted to step foot past the front door. About a week later, after harrying the hotel porter persistently, he informed me that the beauty had left Pärnu; he'd been instructed not to tell me which direction she had taken.

Only then did I comprehend how very deeply I'd fallen in love with her; but it was already late, too late ...

It took about twenty days for the heartbreak to gradually subside, and for me to more or less regain my philosophical composure – essential inner peace for the simple man.

I perceived this when I started noticing the little things in life once again, making my days worth living. When I received a friendly wave from a man with an untamed beard and a sign hung around his neck reading: BUY ME A BEER AND I'LL TELL GOD ABOUT YOU! When I found a new job delivering conscription papers, after being fired from my night watchman's post. When I relearned how to enjoy the rustling of tree leaves, dusk upon the boulevards and the flight of seagulls.

All these things confirmed that I had been accepted again into the brotherhood of life's little joys. And yet ... the world continues to seem somehow emptier and more forlorn. A hushed, almost soundless pain has gnawed at me ever since. The pain is truly miniscule, nearly impossible to perceive, but I can no longer find peace. I suffer for a day, for two or three days, and then have no choice but to drink a little glass or two that dulls the pain at first, then makes things brighter. This continues until I start believing once again that perhaps by way of some miracle, there might still be a chance of rediscovering the midnight-blue beret and winning back the beauty who has already seen it all.

THE HIGH
SEASON

Robert H. was a café poet, mysterious and wilful. And although he wasn't very well-known outside a small circle of experts, we respected him all the more because of it. Upon seeing Robert H. somewhere out on the street, we would nod to him from a distance, always beckoning with calls and gestures for him to join us. In the earlier days, he would occasionally give in to temptation, walking up to us, laughing and chatting for a while. Whenever we asked him where he was from or what he was studying, Robert H. would always reply that the café was his university and his life school. After a while, he ceased responding to our beckoning calls, preferring solitude more and more often. Now and then, he could be seen sitting motionless, wedged into the back corners of cafés and awaiting inspiration, a pencil sharpened to a needlepoint behind his ear and a steaming cup of coffee under his nose.

About a year ago, Robert H. began frequenting the old University of Tartu café more and more often, which was, naturally, only a source of delight for us. But as he had become increasingly more sullen and dour than before, we no longer bothered him with greetings. We simply observed him from a distance, and that was enough for us.

Nevertheless, on rare occasions, usually during a quiet afternoon, it wasn't unknown for him to leap to his feet and start declaiming poetry. Even now, we can still recall one such

reading with crystal clarity, even remembering
the pauses:

> *We drink morning coffee*
> *in silence –*
> *you,   I,*
>   *and death,*
>
> *expressions still drowsy,*
> *just like children's,*
>
> *everyone still has time.*
>
> *Sometime noonish*
> *a window half-ajar*
> *through which we gaze upon*
> *an overgrown garden*
>
> *the rain outside*
> *has just*
> *stopped.*

Whether or not the poem continued somehow, or just ended like that, has escaped my mind. But it was certainly memorable, in any case. So much so that we gave Robert H. a standing ovation – though he apparently didn't enjoy such attention, because he left the café immediately afterward.

Robert H.'s intensifying sullenness worried us somewhat. Sitting and observing his moods, his coffee drinking and his writing had long since become a kind of hobby. There had to be a reason he was so morose. Then, one day, one of us showed up with the joyful news that there truly was: specifically, he'd heard through the grapevine that Robert H.'s high season for a Great Poem had arrived, that the Great Poem was already growing and swelling within him, but its exact delivery date was, as yet, unknown.

This type of news made us alert and, at the same time, cautious, in a heartbeat. We now crept very carefully around Robert H., shadowing the surly poet stealthily and from a distance. We noted that he sat in the old university café more frequently and for longer durations, ultimately favouring a corner table with a big, soft armchair in which he would sit for days at a time. We, the furtive followers of his life's course, occupied places at the opposite end of the café from that point forward, staying and watching from our vantage point in shifts. Only sometimes, rarely, when someone ignorant situated himself too close to Robert H. or – God forbid! – acted so bold as to sit down at the poet's own table, would one of us dash to the sacred side of the café and, with veiled threats, politely ask the ignoramus to leave. One might expect that Robert H. was grateful for it. His agony, caused by the gestation of the Great Poem, was quite obvious.

More and more seldomly did he venture to leave his corner table. In ever-deeper concentration did his ruminative head sink toward his coffee cup. The pencil sharpened to a needlepoint was perched behind his ear; a sheet of white paper lay at the edge of the table like an accusation. This continued until finally, about a week later, it got to the point where Robert H. no longer rose from his place. He became increasingly motionless, and started to slowly fuse to his seat. One time, when Robert H. attempted to stand and fetch a refill, the chair rose into the air along with him; even from the other end of the café, it was clear that his lower back and bottom had *grown into the chair*. A situation such as this forced us to interfere. As Robert H. was no longer able to go buy coffee on his own, we obliquely proposed to him that one of us could serve him at his table for the time being – up until the birth of the Great Poem.

Robert H. glowered as he heard our proposal. He refused any help whatsoever at first, but ultimately relented after mild and incessant entreaties on our part. Hissing tetchily, he demanded that we keep as silent as the grave while serving him, so as not to interrupt his concentration. That, we promised to do.

Our excitement was all-encompassing. Now, we were able to directly assist in the birth of the Great Poem; we were participants in a mystery, the solemn consequence and unanticipated nature of which made us something akin to members of a secret society – so what, that our role was merely to guard Robert H. and serve him coffee! We performed these tasks dutifully and competently. From then on, if any tactless patron of the café started chatting too noisily, or directed undue attention toward Robert H. in any way, failing to realise that a café may also serve as sanctuary for some, we shooed such characters out the door – quietly, without causing a scene. Without interrupting the atmospheric murmur. And one of us would buy Robert H. a new coffee on the hour, setting it on the poet's corner table with a gentle bow, then swiftly withdrawing.

Of course, some of us had to step out of the café from time to time, as we also had our own mundane obligations, along with work and, for some, even a family. At night we were forced to leave Robert H. completely alone in the café, because according to the establishment's rules, only café inventory was allowed to be present during those hours. That did include Robert H., in a sense, because his back and bottom had already fused so seamlessly to the chair over the course of his long wait for the poem that it was no longer possible to separate them without causing injury. Yet Robert H. was so focused on waiting for the Great Poem that this circumstance didn't distress him in the very least.

Nevertheless, the Great Poem was fickle. It just didn't seem to want to come out into the world, and as a result, Robert H. – overheated from the immense amount of coffee he drank – continued melting deeper and deeper into the armchair. This, in turn, meant that after three weeks, it was already quite hard to tell where Robert H. ended and the chair began.

Meanwhile, his upper body had already melted entirely into the upholstery of the chair back, and his lower body had disappeared into the soft seat. The poet's shins had taken the shape of spindly chair legs, leaving the impression that Robert H.'s shoes were now being worn by the chair, not by the man. More or less the same had happened to the poet's head. Robert H.'s neck had already sunk completely into the back of the chair, with only the oval of his face still angling outward. Thus, ultimately, it appeared as though someone had glued a human-faced mask to the chair. Yet that mask still lived and breathed, extremely sensitive to its surroundings, and we had to be on our toes to drive all the gawkers and admirers away from Robert H.'s armchair.

At the same time, our succour for the poet was increased by one more task. Specifically, it became ever more apparent that Robert H. was no longer capable of drinking coffee on his own. His arms and hands, which had been inactive for a month's time, had become almost indistinguishable from the arms of the chair – with the exception of his fingers, which poked out and still allowed him a certain element of anatomical independence. Nevertheless, they couldn't reach the coffee mug. All the same, Robert H. required constant coffee intake so as to not lose alertness. For the Great Poem was like a large animal: it could attack without warning. Up until the final moment, one couldn't be certain which one was stalking which. And so we decided to also take on the responsibility of helping Robert H. drink.

The first time the bravest of us cautiously approached the oval of his face with coffee, Robert H. determinedly pursed his lips and grimaced with his eyebrows and cheeks. But when we carefully made it clear to him that it was in his own interests and crucial for maintaining vigilance, the poet's expression gradually softened; finally, he consented to open his mouth. Sip by sip, with approximately five-minute breaks, he could still manage to empty a cup of coffee in an hour. However, swallowing the beverage was now somewhat more complicated, as Robert H. could no longer turn his head or arch it back. To make sure the last drops didn't go up the poet's nose, we had to tip the chair – or the chair-shaped Robert H., to be exact – a few degrees backward for the final sips.

Nevertheless, the Great Poem kept taking its time.

A few more days passed. Winter was turning to early spring. One would already encounter young, newly enamoured couples strolling on Toome Hill, and the titmice chirruped *city-day-day* from morning to night. One sunny Monday morning, when the café reopened after being closed all day Sunday, we entered with bated breath in the hopes that perhaps Robert H. had delivered the poem. Alas, our hopes were not destined for fulfilment.

We observed in shock that Robert H. was nowhere to be seen. The chair in the corner lacked even the slightest sign of the poet. The shoes were gone from the legs, and neither the oval of his face nor his fingers at the ends of the armrests could be perceived. Had Robert H. truly become one with the chair?

We didn't want to believe it. It couldn't have happened so fast.

We questioned the girl at the register, and the dishwashing girl: it turned out that over the weekend, some kind of banquet had been held at the café, for which all the tables had been pushed together in the middle of the room and the chairs positioned around them. Some foreigners – I think a Danish delegation – had wined and dined there. After the banquet, the tables and chairs had been replaced haphazardly; they were no longer back in the same places they had been before.

"But wasn't it obvious that one chair was wearing shoes?" we asked in exasperation. "Couldn't you see that there was a face sunken into the back of one chair, a focused expression – did that face really not mean anything to you? Or when the delegation sat down at the tables, wasn't there a soft screaming coming from somewhere?"

But the register girl and the dishwashing girl merely shrugged insouciantly at our questions. They hadn't seen or heard a thing.

Poor Robert H., what all might have happened to you that weekend ...?

We discussed what to do next, and decided

to examine all the café chairs one by one. About an hour later, one of us discovered that the back of a chair by the window was slightly bent in the middle, and, for some reason, that bend resembled a nose. Upon closer inspection, having torn away a fair amount of yellow thread, springs and upholstery from the splat, our fingers finally touched a reddish, softly breathing nose. Oh, how our hearts flooded with elation upon seeing it! And when more thread and stitches were pulled away from around the nose, two rheumy, greenish-gray eyes surfaced from the deep cavity in the chair. The eyes could belong only to Robert H. But even more importantly: in spite of the dust and rheum, those eyes twinkled like stars in the heavens! A gaze like that could only emanate from someone in love or overwhelmed by a divine vision. In Robert H.'s case, this could only mean one thing: the Great Poem had arrived at last!

We celebrated like children, laughing, patting each other on the shoulder and winking at Robert to congratulate him on his great achievement. We ordered a round of coffee with cream for everyone in the café, and two cups for Robert H., of course, because he was the one who had exerted himself so. Still, as we sat around a table and began conversing, we gradually turned solemn once again when we realised that Robert no longer had a mouth or hands with which to communicate the poem. Essentially, all that was left of him now was merely a chair – but how do you extract a poem from a chair? We lacked any such experience.

We tore open the upholstery under Robert H.'s nose, hoping he might, perhaps, still have a mouth. And we finally did find something akin to one in the chair back, although the web of threads had already woven so tightly around the lips that parting them by force would certainly have inflicted unbearable pain upon the poet. Some other means of communication had to be found, so we fell into a state of intense contemplation.

Suddenly, an unpleasant buzzing like that of a mosquito sounded from within the chair. It seemed spasmodic, but faintly rhythmic to the keener ear. That is when we realised it was coming from Robert H.'s own mouth: a sound such as that can be produced by blowing through lips pressed tight and stitched together. We noticed that a lower-register whistle was followed by a higher-register one, then a lower and a higher one again. A longer pause intervened, and then it started all over again. What was Robert H. trying to tell us? Was it truly how he was attempting to recite his poem? Observing Robert H. strive to express himself so desperately, a blazing look in his bulging eyes, his quickening breath and certain tremors near the base of the chair, we came to the conclusion that this was, in fact, precisely what he was trying to do. Someone thought to produce a paper and pencil and record the whistles as the poem's rhythmic structure.

About four minutes later, they formed the following pattern on paper:

~ - ~ - ~ - - ~

~ - ~ - ~ - -

~ - ~ - ~ - - ~

~ - ~ - ~ - -

Ultimately, there were a dozen such iambic verse patterns, with pauses between them. A twelve-stanza poem! That's not just a walk in the park. And it appeared that Robert H.

(meaning the chair) had the whole poem memorised word for word. As he whistled the rhythm, his gaze was fixed somewhere far in the distance – as far off as only poets can manage to stare – where it seemed like he was watching each and every word soar by. Gradually, the impact of the Great Poem also sunk into its listeners. One of us leaned thoughtfully against the wall, his cheek resting on his fist; another collapsed between the tables in soft astonishment; a third buried his teary face into his hands; a fourth opened his mouth for a sickly sneeze; the mouth of a fifth gaped in euphoric laughter; a sixth was thunderstruck by the fact that he wasn't thunderstruck ... the Great Poem left no one feeling indifferent.

After finishing his poem, or rather his ecstatic whistling march, Robert H. rapidly veered toward the opposite extreme. His eyes became misty with drowsiness, and his breathing almost ceased entirely.

We stayed at his side until that evening, watching mournfully as the armchair gradually swallowed the poet until not even the bulge of his nose remained. Or was that just how the café, the Great Café World, had received him? What spaces, what smells, what light awaited him ahead? We didn't know. We could only speculate. And before we left, finding that we'd done everything we were obliged to do on this side, we ordered another round of large coffees for every table, to remember and pay tribute to our friend, the poet Robert H.

Adam Cullen (b. 1986) is a translator of Estonian literature into English. His translations include two novels nominated for the Cultural Endowment of Estonia's Prize for Literary Translation: Mihkel Mutt's *The Cavemen Chronicle* (2015) and Rein Raud's *The Brother and the Reconstruction* (2017). His first collection of original poetry, *Lichen/Samblik*, was published in 2017. Originally from Minnesota, USA, he has resided in Estonia since 2007.

Tiina Randviir (b. 1952) was born in Tallinn. After graduating from the University of Tartu, she worked for many years in the publishing industry. She has translated a number of authors into Estonian, including Alessandro Baricco, Italo Calvino, Carlo Collodi, Elena Ferrante, Helen Fielding and Brigid Keenan.

New titles from Paper + Ink

O. Henry
The Gift of the Magi & Other Stories

Guy de Maupassant
The Necklace & Other Stories

Oscar Wilde
The Happy Prince & Other Stories

D. H. Lawrence
The Rocking Horse Winner & Other Stories

Mark Twain
*The Celebrated Jumping Frog of Calaveras County
& Other Stories*

Žemaitė
Tofylis, or The Marriage of Zosė
Translated from the Lithuanian by Violeta Kelertas

Rūdolfs Blaumanis
In the Shadow of Death
Translated from the Latvian by Uldis Balodis

Visit **www.paperand.ink** to subscribe and receive the other books
by post, as well as to keep up to date about new volumes in the series.